Sailaway Home

BRUCE DEGEN

SCHOLASTIC INC.
New York

Copyright © 1996 by Bruce Degen   All rights reserved. Published by Scholastic Inc.
SCHOLASTIC HARDCOVER is a registered trademark of Scholastic Inc.
No part of this publication may be reproduced in whole or in part, or stored in a retrieval system,
or transmitted in any form or by any means, electronic, mechanical, photocopying, recording, or
otherwise, without written permission of the publisher.
For information regarding permission, write to Scholastic Inc., 555 Broadway, New York, NY 10012.
Library of Congress Cataloging-in-Publication Data
Degen, Bruce.   Sailaway home / by Bruce Degen.   p. cm.
    Summary: A young pig imagines fantastic adventures in the sky and sea, always being able to return
    home at day's end.
ISBN 0-590-46443-4   [1. Pigs — Fiction. 2. Imagination — Fiction. 3. Stories in rhyme.] I. Title.
PZ8.3.D364Sai 1996   [E] — dc20   95-15737   CIP   AC
12 11 10 9 8 7 6 5 4 3 2 1   6 7 8 9/9 0 1/0
Printed in the United States of America   First printing, April 1996
The illustrator used pen and ink, watercolor, color pencil, and gouache
for the paintings in this book.
Production supervision by Angela Biola
Designed by Claire B. Counihan

For Sam

Sailaway, sailaway,
Over the foam.

Blow with the gale away,
Bail with a pail away,

Hitch to a whale, and then
Sailaway home.

Rideaway, rideaway,
Where will you roam?

Where pirates hide away,

With treasures to pry away,

Slipaway, slide, and then
Rideaway home.

Flyaway, flyaway,
Up in the sky away.

Cloud beds to lie away,

Rainbow cream pie away,

Cut me a slice, and then . . .

Flyaway home.

Skipaway, skipaway,
Out on my own.

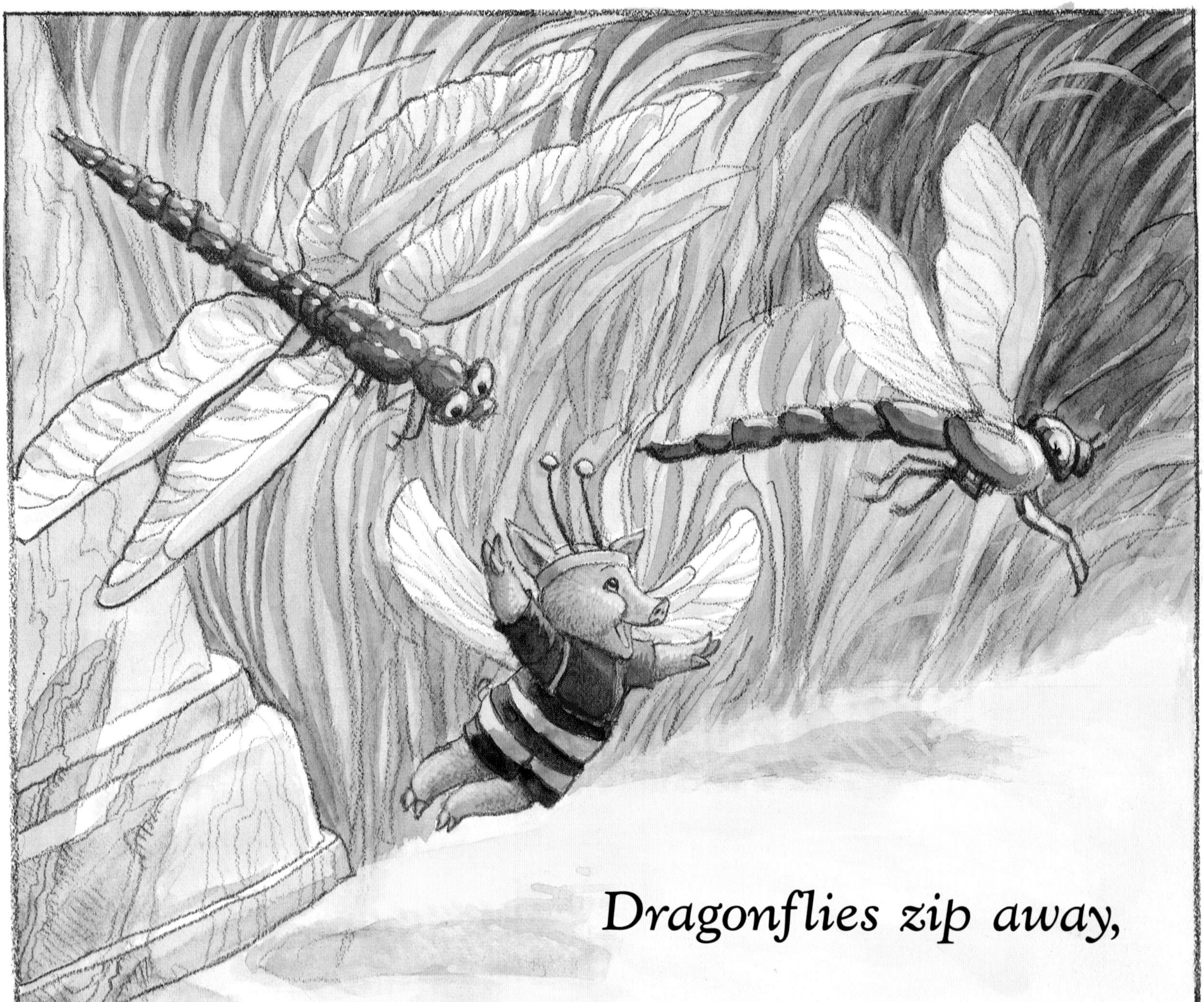

Dragonflies zip away,

Butterflies sip away,

Frogs do a flip, and then
Skipaway home.

Runaway, runaway,

Happy alone.

Dreams in the sun away,
Battles all won away,
There's someone to tell
if you . . .

Runaway home.